Revers

Who'd have believed it?

We went from being a nearly dead-in-the-water, over-the-hill, lifeless has-been outfit to being a mean and motivated crack operation overnight.

And it was all because of a girl.

Well, not a girl, exactly, but Vanessa, which was close enough.

#5

THE WOLF GANG

Also by Chris Lynch

THE
WOLF GANG

Chris Lynch

📖 HarperTrophy®
A Division of HarperCollinsPublishers

The Wolf Gang
Copyright © 1998 by Chris Lynch
All rights reserved. No part of this book may be used or reproduced in any
manner whatsoever without written permission except in the case of brief
quotations embodied in critical articles and reviews. Printed in the United
States of America. For information address HarperCollins Children's
Books, a division of HarperCollins Publishers,
10 East 53rd Street, New York, NY 10022.

Library of Congress Cataloging-in-Publication Data
Lynch, Chris.
  The Wolf Gang / Chris Lynch.
    p.   cm. — (The He-Man Women Haters Club ; #5)
  Summary: The members of the He-Man Women Haters Club attempt
to restore it to its former glory when a rival club with female members
emerges.
  ISBN 0-06-440659-8(pbk.).— ISBN 0-06-027418-2 (lib. bdg.)
  [1. Clubs—Fiction. 2. Sex role—Fiction. 3. Humorous stories.]
I. Title. II. Series: Lynch, Chris. He-Man Women Haters Club ; #5.
PZ7.L979739Wo 1998   97-41954
[Fic]—dc21   CIP
                                                          AC

1   2   3   4   5   6   7   8   9   10
❖
First Edition

Contents

1
The Continuing Legend of J. Chesthair

Johnny's back.

How many disasters did it take before everyone realized there could be only one true leader of the He-Man Women Haters Club, and that leader was old Johnny Chesthair himself?

Can I say it again?

Johnny Chesthair, back on top.

So maybe I'm gloating a little. But I'm sitting in the big chair, and the big chair feels good.

I never should have left it. Here's how it happened.

I started with a big car and a big dream, to gather up all the right-thinking, two-fisted, red-blooded, big-muscley . . .

No, scratch that. I started with Jerome. And it wasn't even my idea. It was Jerome's. He put into my head that it might be kind of awesome to get together a lot of macho guys like me, who would hang with me, and act like me, and talk like me, and listen to me. . . .

Sounds like paradise, no? Right, it sounded that way to me, too. But then Jerome—whose whole problem is that he doesn't look or act or do anything much like me and doesn't have so much as a single hair on his chest—came with his own little set of quirks. Like, he quits the club every fifteen minutes because some small thing or other is brushing his fur the wrong way. And girls harass him—like, pelt him with snowballs, or kiss him against his will, or stalk him—pretty much around the clock. Jerome is our high-maintenance He-Man. And on top of that, he went on his own and advertised for new members. He put out his little bulletin on—ready?—on the Internet.

I know, I know. But he did it before I could stop him.

The result was Ling-Ling.

Ling weighs in at a cool seven thousand pounds (with a hat on, because he would be naked without some lunatic headgear at all times). He towers over even me, and cries like a faucet if you give him half a reason. Like if you wear red on a Wednesday, that might set him off . . . or eat your fries before your burger, and watch him flood. He's a very sensitive He-Man. But then, he's watched the movie *Patton* six million times, reads those crazy commando gun magazines as if they're the FAO Schwarz catalog, and is so far deep into superhero comics that he even became one for a while. Bolt Upright. How's that sound? Pretty heroic, don't you think? Pretty sane? Not a whole lot, no.

Ling should wear one of those signs that say, "Caution, do not touch. Third rail is *live!*"

Then we got a hick from Alabama named Cecil. Cecil is very nice.

What? What? I didn't say anything else. Cecil is very nice.

All right, so he's also roughly as smart as your average soup bone. But don't knock it. There is not a better recruit in the world than a loyal, strong, simpleminded goofball who also happens to look just like Abraham Lincoln without a beard, and is handy with a hammer and nail.

Anyway, cunning and intelligence aren't everything. In fact, sometimes they can become a problem.

A serious problem.

Which brings us to the other guy.

Those I've mentioned already, those are the good ones. Good guys. Good people. Good He-Men.

Then there's the other one.

His name is Wolfgang. His mother knew what she was doing when she named him (if he ever even *had* a mother, which I think is unlikely). Because while he isn't a wolf, and he isn't a gang, he makes as much trouble as any pack of wild dogs ever could.

He's in a wheelchair. But don't be fooled.

It's an unfortunate story, since Wolf was one of the original four members of the He-Man Women Haters Club. He was even president for a while, and turned us into a very successful rock-and-roll band. You probably read about us. And despite the fact that he was always picking fights with me for no reason (and of course I had to let him win sometimes, because of the legs thing), he made a pretty tough and useful He-Man.

But then they got him.

Women.

The dark side of the force.

Now he is no longer a He-Man—he is the enemy. We had a trial and ran him out. He thinks he quit, but he is mistaken. We showed mercy. We did not impose the death penalty.

That was our fatal mistake. Our kindness was our weakness.

2
Her Satanic Majesty

Can I just interrupt for one minute, please? There have been, by my estimation, about twelve thousand lies perpetuated about me by now by Johnny Chipmunk, and I'd like to address this.

Oh, I'm the devil. I'm so scary. I'm so mean. Boo-hoo.

Couldn't you just slap him sometimes?

Hello, I'm Monica, in case you couldn't tell, and like, what have I ever done to him that was so bad? Sure, I kissed him one time. Did he not kiss me back? Oh yes, he did indeed, the little fish lip. Not only did he do it and like it, he was so excited about the event, he treated my lip to an experience I'm sure only a spoonful of Jell-O would understand. And he drooled. Right onto the bib of my practically-new-this-year Girl Scout uniform, laminating a half-dozen badges. He was like he just came from the dentist with half a Novocained face.

The boy can't kiss and salivate at the same time—and I don't even want to think about why a person would feel the need to do those two things simultaneously. There's something very wrong there, I think.

If only he didn't have that face.

You know the way butterscotch pudding feels? Exactly. If butterscotch pudding were a face, it would be Steven's face.

I said that at the dinner table one night and my father said, "Oh ya? Well, when I see him, I'm going to get the world's biggest can of that nitrogen-propelled whipped cream, and I'm going to take Butterscotch Boy and . . ."

Ya, ya, ya, Dad. Can somebody tell me why guys talk like that? Especially when everybody knows they're just big fat cream puffs who wouldn't even—

You know, whenever I talk about guys, I always compare them to food. More often than not dessert items. I wonder why that is.

I will tell you very simply the difference between boys and girls (and I wish Johnny Chestnut would ask me so I could straighten him out and we could get down to business): When a girl wants something, she moves first one leg and then the other, plants foot A, then foot B, and pretty soon she has reached the object she desires; when a boy wants something, he . . . jumps on his motorcycle or his monster bigfoot truck or his aircraft carrier or whatever big toy is hot that week, and he beats it as far and as fast as he can *away* from the thing he desires. And he hopes it followed him.

Also, guys don't ask questions. Girls do. I ask questions, do I not? It's the only way to find out things. You know what a guy does when he doesn't know something? He makes a proclamation. "Atmospheric conditions in this part of the country make it categorically impossible to tell what conditions will be like," is what a guy would say, when a girl would ask, "Is it supposed to rain tomorrow?"

Other than that, I think we're pretty much alike.

Anyway, so he kissed me, and what's more, he's going to do it again. You see, I have joined a particular club . . . and my club and his club are destined to spend a great deal of time together.

And next time, he'd better bring both lips.

Now you can go back to listening to his fantasies. If you're feeling stupid, go right ahead and believe him.

3
Gangin' Up

"The stupidest thing I ever saw," I said.

"No, Steven," Cecil responded. "I think it's pretty darn decent of ol' Wolfgang. He wants to still be friends in spite of what-all you done to him."

"What *I* did? To *him*? Listen, that guy spent his whole time here just trying to mess up my life and my club, and now that he's out, he's still trying. Well, I say, nothing doing."

We were at the club, hanging out, doing nothing much but sitting in, on, or under my beautiful black Lincoln. No heavy lifting, no major brain-wave motion disrupting things. Just the way a guy likes it.

Until the mail came. Now, understand that in the six months or so the He-Man Women Haters Club had been in existence, we had previously received three pieces of mail: First, Ling received his induction notice telling him he'd been drafted into the Greek Army (I warned him that the free-knife offer he answered at the back of his magazine was going to be a trick); the twelve boxes of Girl Scout cookies we never ordered arrived along with a big fat bill; and somebody sent Wolfgang a "Happy Birthday" singing-belly-dancer telegram. (He said it was from Bill Clinton; we said it was from himself.)

So when a piece of mail came to Lars's garage addressed to the HMWHC, we noticed. And when the return address read THE WOLF GANG, we ducked.

"You want me to dunk it in water for you?" Lars asked. "They can do them letter-bomb things these days, you know. And that cripple boy, he's a clever one . . . and a mean and scary one, I don't mind tellin' you now that he's gone. Never never liked him, never trusted him at all."

"Really?" asked Jerome in his I-think-I'll-insult-Steven's-uncle-and-he-won't-even-know-it voice. "You were licking his wheels pretty good when you wanted to be in our rock-and-roll band. So what was it you didn't like about Wolfgang, Lars, his brain?"

"Exactly," Lars said, as if the two of them were agreeing.

"Stop picking on Lars," I snapped.

"What?" Lars asked. "Who's pickin'?"

"Never mind," I answered. "Just give me the letter. I'm not afraid of any letter bomb *he* could send me anyhow."

I tore it open with my teeth, to the gape-mouthed amazement of my troops.

"What a stupid name anyway," I said before reading. "The Wolf Gang. Pathetic. You'd think he could at least come up with a tougher-sounding . . ."

"Like He-Man," Jerome prodded, "or Johnny Chesthair."

"Don't get fresh," I said.

I read the letter out loud (after a quick silent run-through to make sure there were no tricky three- or four-syllable words lurking in there):

Dear Comrades,

Even though you guys tried to railroad me and court-martial me and hang me by the neck until dead, I hold no hard feelings. As a matter of fact I've been thinking, as I kick back in the comfort of my impressive new clubhouse, what a shame it is that we can't all be together again. We sure had some rockin' times back there in the early days of the club, before you got all screwed up. I'd like to try and make things better, because I am a big person, and extend to your club an invitation to come visit me and mine at my new club, The Wolf Gang. Don't you love the name?

Anyway, I have to go now, very busy Wolf-banging around, you see. But please come by next Saturday, take the tour, have a cold Yoo-Hoo, and renew old times.

> *Sincere as always,*
> *Prince Wolfgang I*
> *Absolute Ruler*
> *Defender of the Faith*
> *Chief Executive Officer*
> *Party Guy*
> *Sacred Order of the Gang*
> *of Wolf*

P.S. If Steven is too afraid to come, I understand.

Oh, boy oh boy, can Wolfgang chew a raw nerve like a dog on a ham bone, or what? Afraid? Me? Of *him?* That'll be the day. That . . . will . . . be . . . the . . . day. I don't fear him, I just hate him. There's a great big difference. But he wouldn't understand that.

"Can you believe this cheese ball?" I said to my troops. "Trying to say that I, Johnny Chesthair, am afraid of a rat like him. . . . Get a load of this guy, will ya? He'll say anything to get attention."

I laughed my patented brave laugh. Laughed it long, laughed it hard.

Laughed it alone.

"What?" I said when I realized my boys were a little skeptical. "What? You don't *buy* it, do you?"

"Well," Jerome answered gently, "Wolf always did have a way of getting to you."

"*Getting* to me, sure, because he was such a slime bag. But that's not the same as—"

"And there were all those fights," Ling said. "With Wolfgang . . . that you . . . well . . . didn't win."

Lars rushed to my defense. Good man, Lars. Good uncle.

"Well, of course, what kind of a guy do you think Steven is? He was raised right. Why, I can't tell you how many times I was over to his house for supper and his old man, my brother, pointed his knife across the table and said, 'Boy, whatever you do in this life, don't you never beat up on no cripples. That, and never look at another guy in the gym shower. Those are the two things.' So of course Steven never beat up on Wolfgang, he lost on purpose. Because he was raised Christian."

Excellent story, even if I didn't recall Lars ever being to my house for dinner. Even when they went bowling together, my dad made him wait on the steps.

"But it is all right, ain't it?" Cecil asked naively. "For a guy to be afraid once in a while? I mean, sometimes, bein' afraid just makes sense."

I was back in charge of the club now, so it was my job to provide this kind of guidance.

"No, it is not all right. We do not be afraid. It does not make sense. It is not allowed."

"Well," Cecil went on, "forgive me for bein' simple here, but seems to me that you break your own rule sometimes. 'Cause the way you act all panicky and deranged whenever that girl Monica—"

"That's *different*!" I blurted. "That's not fear, that's confusion. Because she is a deceptive and unpredictable opponent who plays by no known set of rules, and who will stoop as low as humanly possible to bring down her enemy. That is confusion, not fear. Confusion. Not fear. Confusion . . ."

Cecil was satisfied, even impressed, with my response. Not so the others. Ling shook his head dubiously. Jerome openly laughed at me.

"What's your problem?" I asked.

13

"Her *enemy? You* are her enemy?" Jerome asked. "Steven, if what Monica does to you is how she treats her enemies, what does she do when she *likes* somebody? Fetch their slippers with her teeth? Throw money at them? Lay her coat over mud puddles for them to walk over?"

You cannot reason with Jerome when he gets like this. You have to just move on. "Obviously," I said calmly, "you have fallen for her ploy."

"Colonel?" Ling called with his hand raised.

Now, here was a He-Man I could talk to. I acknowledged him with a regal nod.

"I hate to disagree with you, but it just seems, from the way your hand is shaking with that letter in it, and the way your eyes keep rolling all the way back in your head every time anyone mentions Wolfgang . . ."

God, I hated the sound of that name.

". . . Ya, just like you're doing right now. Well, sir, this would seem to indicate that it may be true, that you harbor a little fear of Wolf."

"That is not fear!" I insisted once more. "That is anger. Anger is good. And it is rage. Rage is good. Anger and rage are good. They make a guy strong. They are good. They are good, not fear. Fear bad. Anger, rage good."

Apparently, that didn't come out the way I'd intended it. The three of them stared back at me with even more concern than before I started explaining.

"Fine," I snapped. "We'll go to the stupid Wolf stupid Gang stupid Club and take the stupid tour and drink a stupid Yoo-stupid-Hoo and then you'll see that stupid Wolf and his stupid Gang don't bother me at all. Is that what you want? You want to put Johnny to the test?"

They shrugged and nodded at the same time, all three of them. A forceful, decisive outfit, my men.

"Okay," I said. "Just you remember, the last time we let what's-his-gang lead us blindly into a powwow, we were ambushed into . . ."

I paused, forced my voice down into the very bottom of its manly range.

". . . a *dance party*," I rumbled.

A chill went through the room.

4
The Aquamarine Door

Unless we had the wrong address, things were taking a turn for the ugly here.

The four of us stood there on the sidewalk, staring up at the sign: YVETTE'S HAIR—MANICURE—PEDICURE—AROMATHERAPY.

"This can't be right," Jerome said.

"I *hope* it's not right," Ling said.

"Pedicure," Cecil mused. "Does it got somethin' to do with animals? 'Cause it sure don't smell like no animals in there."

He was right about that. Coming out of Yvette's Hair were the mingled smells of nail polish, shampoo, lavender, lemon, mint, apple, chamomile, incense, licorice, and a hundred other oily warm scents.

"Boys," I said darkly, "breathe it in deep and get to know that smell. That is the smell of evil right there."

Jerome laughed at me, but cut himself off quickly when the shop's glass door opened and the little bell above it tinkled. Then smart-boy Jerome scurried behind me.

"Hello," the tall lady said happily. "I couldn't help noticing four handsome young men standing in front of my window."

I spread my arms wide in a protective gesture, with my men huddling behind me. "Get back, boys," I announced. "It's a trap."

The tall lady laughed without bothering to hide it from me. "Aha," she said. "You must be Steven."

As I feared, the big ones are just as spooky as the little ones.

"I'm sorry, sir, but we don't do chesthair."

And just as vicious.

I turned on my men. "The first one who laughs . . ."

Jerome fitted his whole fist into his mouth to cork himself.

"The kids are around back," she said. "Through the alley entrance, the aquamarine door."

We backed away as a group. When we were a safe distance from Yvette, we turned and ran around the corner.

Standing in front of the entrance to Wolf's club-house, in all her brutal glory, was Ling's big (big, big) sister, Rock. She had one great paw resting on one meaty hip, and the other curled around her javelin. She held the spear at her side, like a centurion guard standing in front of the palace in an old gladiator movie.

"So, we meet again," I said. You can't let them get in the first shot.

"Wanna be impaled?" she asked good-naturedly.

"Don't, Steven," Ling said. "It hurts. It hurts a lot."

It made sense that she should stand there looking like a palace guard. Because that's what Wolf's club was, a palace. A puff palace.

There were two rooms, not counting the front where Yvette did her evil business. The first room, coming from the back through the aquamarine door, was for storage and . . . I don't know, the reception area, I guess.

"Would you like a cup of tea?"

"What?" I jumped back toward the door. She'd come out of nowhere. I knew her from somewhere but couldn't figure it out. She looked normal enough, for a girl—long brown hair, jeans, white sweatshirt—but something wasn't right about her. Like she was in disguise.

"No," I snapped. "I don't want any tea, and neither do they." I pointed at my men not with a finger, but with my whole fist. "We don't *do* tea."

She shook her head at me. "You need a *lot* of help, kid."

"Oh ya," Cecil jumped in. "Well, maybe he does . . ."

We all waited for him to finish.

No, that was it. He was finished.

"Thanks, Cecil," I said. He nodded.

So there were at least two women in Wolf's new club. He was sinister, boy.

"Have a seat," Rock said, pointing at a contraption that was either a retired piece of hairdressing equipment or a boy-killing death device. It was like a sofa, covered in peach vinyl, but with four gigantic helmetlike hoods hovering above each of the seating positions.

"Right," Ling said, challenging his big sister. "We sit down there, those things come down over our heads, and then what? Is it an electrical charge that gets us, or a poison gas, or are spikes going to come down and shoot through our heads?"

"They're hair dryers, stupid."

"Heh-heh-heh," Ling said. "Better men than me

have fallen for the old 'just a hair dryer' line."

"Better men than you have fallen for 'Hey, your shoe's untied,'" Rock said as she shoved him down into the seat. It didn't actually kill him, so Cecil sat too. Then Jerome.

"Actually, I'd love a cup of tea," Jerome said.

"Coming right up," the other girl said. "You sure you won't have a seat and a cup of tea?" she asked me again as she headed for the office door.

"I don't drink," I said. "And I don't sit. Ever."

She nodded. "That explains a lot."

The four of us remained silent under the watchful eye of Rock as we waited for his majesty to see us. Another girl came out and served Jerome. *Another* one, not the one who had taken his order. Jerome was shaken, looking up at her.

"I know that one," he said as she walked away. "I remember her from the snowballing incident. She is one of the—"

"Girl Scouts," I growled.

"This is starting to smell like another setup," Ling said. "Steven, I think we better run!"

He jumped up out of his seat and bumped into a stack of metal shelves holding cans of hair spray, jelly jars of green goop, mousse and cream and nail polish . . . hundreds and hundreds of bottles of nail polish in hundreds and hundreds of shades. Enough polish to lacquer the claws of an army of girl soldiers. Or one gigantic killer fingernail that could skewer us all at once.

Jerome and Cecil jumped up too. Jerome spilled his tea. Rock laughed. The boys broke for the aquamarine door, threw it open . . . and jumped back from it when a column of several more out-of-uniform Girl Scouts marched in.

"So you want to play rough," I said, rolling up my sleeves. "This is it, guys . . . it's our Little Big Horn!"

At that point the office door flew open, and everyone turned.

"General Custer," Wolf said in that old smooth tone of his. "I am so happy you could come."

He rolled into the room, being pushed along by his right-hand man.

Mmmm*mon*ic-c-c-c-ca.

It had reached the point where I couldn't even *think* her name without stuttering.

"Hey, Wolfgang," Cecil said with a big wave, as if Wolf was not the enemy.

"Huckleberry, how are ya?" Wolf said, waving him on for a big hug.

Jerome watched the embrace from a distance.

Wolf, catching his eye from over Cecil's shoulder, laughed.

"Jerome, my old and dear friend. How good to see you again after all this time."

"I just saw you like a week ago at the Store 24."

"Jeez, it seems like so much longer. And Ling, you old rascal. All my friends, all my comrades, together again. This just makes me so . . . happy . . . I think I'm gonna cry."

All right, *crying* now, for crying out loud. He is a genius, in his demented way. Here he was inviting us into his new club, which was the photographic negative of his old club, and taking all the things we stood for—no girls, no tea, no crying—and making a mockery of them.

"Have the girls been taking care of you all right there, Steve-o?" he asked. "You comfortable? Anything you need?"

"No, I'm all—"

"Here," Wolf said. "Have a cookie."

The monster.

"I don't want a cookie," I growled.

"Sure you do. We've got them all. We've got your Tagalongs, your Samoas, your Thin Mints. . . ."

Every Girl Scout cookie there was. He gestured to a separate unit of shelves that held nothing but the cookies, every variety at least five or six boxes deep.

"You keep your rotten cookies away from me," I said.

They all hissed, and went *oooohhh* in mock fear of me.

"See?" Monica said to her new boss. "I told you he'd just be weird."

"Now, now," Wolf said to her. "Steven's not weird. He just doesn't act like any other person any of us have ever met before. Steve-o and I go way, way back. We had some rootin'-tootin' times together, and I don't want to spoil all that now."

Cecil raised his hand.

"But, ah, we did try and court-martial you and stuff last time we was all together."

Wolf waved him off. "All in good fun, though."

I couldn't take any more of this. "All right, what's your game?"

"What?" he said innocently. "Game? What game?"

"*Your* game. What's your angle? You always have one."

"All right," he said. "You got me. I have a motive. I want us all to be one big happy family again. I want my club and your club to join in a

23

partnership, to forge a truce and bridge our gap and—"

"You don't even have one single guy in your club," I said, sounding as if there was a dead cow decaying in the middle of their clubhouse and nobody would clean it up.

"I know, I know. And to tell you the truth, I thought I would like it, but I feel an emptiness. I miss the camaraderie we used to have over at the Women Haters."

The Girl Scout gallery booed.

"So what I propose is that we get together, all of us, to make us all stronger."

I laughed in his face.

"I see you want some time to think about it," he said. "Why don't I take you on a tour of our facility while we talk about it?"

"Hah," I scoffed. "This ought to be good for a laugh."

Wolf nodded at Monica, who then went to the door that led into the front of the shop. She opened the door and stuck her head in. "Mom, is it okay if we come through now?"

I knew there was something not right about that Yvette.

Monica waved us on in, and we followed.

As we took the tour, following behind Monica's mom as she showed us the shampooing station, the cutting station, the drying station, etc., Wolfgang drifted farther and farther toward the back of the group, pulling me along with him. Finally we left the group altogether, winding up in his office. It was a very bare, cold, and colorless room compared to the other two. I liked it right off.

He whispered as we faced each other across his desk—which had a nameplate on it that read YVETTE. "See, what I figure is, you guys can just join up, no questions asked. Kind of like an introductory offer, limited time, no fees, that kind of thing. Because I know you guys. Of course, you'll have to dump the old name, since it really is kind of out-of-date anyhow and it offends some of my membership, as you can imagine, and—tell the truth—you all never really hated women anyway. So we'll all just be in the Wolf Gang from this point on."

That was it, that was Wolfgang all the way. He was absolute wickedness like straight out of the Bible or *Star Wars*—the soldier from the side of goodness who fell, then turned right around to come and take the rest of the good guys down with him.

He smiled for me his rottenest smile ever, and stuck out his hand like we'd just finalized some dirty deal.

"You're crazy, Wolfgang, you know that?" I stood up, looking down over his desk. "Nuts. Why don't you just give it up and stay here playing dolls with your new little friends? We kicked you out of the club because you were no good, and you're not getting back in no matter how sneaky you are about it."

"Steven, Steven, Steven," he said. I hate it when he calls me that. "All I want is to help you."

He sounded so calm and sure of himself that I knew I had to get out of there right that minute. I burst out through the door and heard the rubber of his wheels as he took off after me.

I ran out into the front of the shop to collect my men.

Horrors! How could I have fallen for it? I never should have left them out there unprotected.

Cecil was sitting in the shampooing chair, reclined to full horizontal position, as Yvette massaged his scalp. Ling was sitting in a chair completely dazed, as if he'd been hypnotized or drugged, as Monica opened up one little vial after another and waved each one under his nose.

"Now smell this one," she said seductively. "Doesn't it make you think of the beach and wildflowers? Don't the muscles in your neck just start to . . ."

Jerome.

Jerome!

My god, no.

Jerome was sitting right up there in the front window, across a small table from a small woman in a white lab coat. The woman spoke softly to him, held his hand, and buffed his nails with a white Popsicle stick.

"You see," she said, "real men get this all the time. There is nothing in the world wrong with wanting the small details of your personal appearance to be in order. It is actually a sign of strength . . . and you have such fine, big strong hands. . . ."

Jerome's hands are roughly the size and strength of butterfly wings.

"What is going on here?" I yelled. It looked like the *Wizard of Oz* scene when the Scarecrow, Tin Man, and Lion were getting all primped up to meet the Wizard. "On your feet, men. We're getting out of here right now. And we're going out the *front* door."

I marched. Cecil and Ling snapped out of their trances and fell in line behind me.

"God, you are so uptight, Johnny Fishlips," Monica said. She pointed one of her potions at me. "*You* could use aromatherapy more than anyone else I know. Here, come over here and smell this."

"No, *you* smell this," I said.

She waited. "Good one, Johnny," she said.

It wasn't until we were outside and half a block down the street that we realized Jerome was not with us.

"My god," Ling gasped. "We left a man behind enemy lines!"

We bolted back to the shop, then were stopped short to find him still sitting there in the front window. The woman was now working on his other hand as he admired the high polish of the first.

"He-Man Jerome," I barked as I stuck my head in the door under the tinging bell. "Come on, we're outta here."

He looked up at me, then back at his manly manicure.

"She said she did General Colin Powell's nails once."

"I'll slap your face," Ling ranted. "General

28

Powell is one of the greatest—"

"Jerome!" I yelled again, hoping the recognition of his own name might bring him back. "Let's go, man."

His words came slowly, thickly. He stared at his nails. She was massaging the spaces between his knuckles now, and you could almost hear him purr.

"I will, Steven," Jerome said. "I'll be right there. She's just going to finish doing this hand, and then I'll be right along. You go on ahead."

I never would have believed it. Not He-Man Jerome. No, no, not Jerome.

As we retreated again, I caught a glimpse of Wolf, the four-wheeled devil himself, watching and smiling from the darkness of his back-room empire.

5
Guerrilla Girlfriend

Broke my He-Man heart.

It was the saddest sight of my life, watching Jerome's very essence being bled out of him by that cult of females Wolf calls a club. Maybe that's how they do it, through the fingernails, sucking the strength and manliness right out of a guy and leaving him a wreck, a shell, a broken wasted joke. Poor He-Man Jerome.

Jerome, ya broken, wasted joke.

"Really?" Cecil asked when I gave the boys that good-bye Jerome memorial speech back at the garage. "If you ask me, he looked happier than I ever seen him. Shows y'all what I know, huh?"

"Yes, it does," I said.

"You are so right, Steven," Lars said. "That's just exactly the way they work it. They lull you into a state of reduced awareness by hypnotizing you or feeding you real good food or singing, right, then they take all your power away. Like when Samson got all his hair cut off. So ya should just stay away from 'em altogether, or next thing ya know they'll be taking every hair off your chest with Nair while you're asleep in front of the TV, or they'll trick ya into talking baby talk to 'em while they're secretly recording it to play for their friends, or . . ."

The problem with Lars was, there seemed to be so much history back there between him and some woman or women that he always wound up giving us more information than we would ever want to know.

"But we can't just quit on Jerome, can we?" Ling asked. "I mean, don't we owe it to him to try and save him? Come on, Steven, he was your first recruit, your comrade, and you're going to leave him there behind enemy lines?"

Sometimes if you listen to Ling, he can really get you thinking straight. Not often, but sometimes.

"We can't let it happen," I said. "Our boy is in trouble, and Wolf is getting more dangerous every day. Power. Authority. Some people are built to handle it—like myself. Others just shouldn't be allowed."

Ling nodded. "War. There is no other solution. It can't be avoided."

I agreed. "Wolf has just gotten too mighty over there. And we, as everyone knows, are men of action."

So we were sitting around after making the declaration of war, trying to figure out exactly what that meant. Our first move was to take the meeting into the War Room.

Ling spoke in hushed tones, looking over his shoulder even though we were in the safety of our own Lincoln in the middle of our own locked garage. "I have a magazine that has an ad, in the back . . . where we can get *actual* nuclear weapons. If we can scare up $49.95 plus shipping and handling."

Lars had been eavesdropping outside the car. He threw open the door, pushed his way in next to Cecil on the backseat. I was driving—naturally— and Ling was riding shotgun—also naturally.

"Well, that's just stupid," Lars said about the warhead proposition. I was very surprised by my uncle's unusual attack of common sense. I shouldn't have been. "Because," he went on, "if you nuke their clubhouse, it's so close, you'll get all that nuke-u-lar dust floating back here to your own place. And that's no good. Everybody knows you need to be far away from a nuke-u-lar event, like when Three Mile Island melted, but I was livin' practically a half a mile away so I comed out all good."

Lars scratched his forehead with his elbow and looked around at us. "Was I finished?"

"Ya," I said. "Thanks." When he'd left us, I got back to the point. "I was thinking more like we'd toilet-paper the beauty shop, fill their aroma-therapy bottles with ammonia, something like that."

"I know," Cecil contributed. "Let's make hair-cut appointments . . . and not show up!"

He was giggling, rubbing his hands together, proud and silly at the same time.

"And that, Ladies and Gentlemen, is why they call him The Killer," I said. He blushed.

"We can't do any of that," Ling said. "Our fight's with the Wolf Gang. If we bother Yvette, we'll get in trouble."

"Trouble?" I asked. "Not like if we nuked 'em, huh? That wouldn't bother anybody, you don't suppose?"

So we were pretty much back where we started,

which was no place. We were kidding ourselves. War? What did we possibly know about launching a—

"Lemme in!" came the screechy voice from the street.

We didn't answer, just turned to stare in the direction of the voice.

"Lemme in! Lemme in! Lemme in right now!" the screech went on, accompanied by a wild rattling and pounding of the door.

"Gee," Cecil remarked, "ever since we locked the door, everybody wants to get in all of a sudden."

"Go away," I hollered.

"I won't!" it hollered back.

"Don't make me come out there," I called.

"Don't make me come in there," it called back.

I turned to Ling and shrugged. Ling got out of the car and walked to the door. Putting on a voice almost as large as his body, he bellowed, "Apparently you don't know who you're fooling with in here, kid, but if you go quietly, we won't come after you until you've had a sporting head start. We are the He-Man—"

Even *with* a sporting head start, we probably wouldn't go after the kid. But we did get out of the car to stand behind our leader.

"Ah, it's the fat one? You got your cape on in there? That what you boys do all day, fly around inside a locked garage? Open this door or I'll chew my way in and kick you so hard you will land on the planet Krypton."

Ling started running backward away from the door. "Oh god, Steven, it's Vanessa." He barreled— much faster than he could run in forward gear—all the way back to the Lincoln and dove inside. All the while he kept staring at the door as if Vanessa was going to bore her way through like the thing in *Aliens*.

Not that He-Man Ling's afraid of her, now. He just doesn't like her much, that's all.

"Nessy?" Cecil called, hopping back into the car beside Ling. "That's the little mean one, ain't it?"

I stood there in the middle of the garage, my hands on my hips. "I just want to tell you guys what an honor it is to be associated with you. No, really."

Alone, I walked across the garage to face the fierce Nessy—through a bolted door.

"What do you want here, Ness?" I growled.

"Yo, Johnny Chestcold," she said. "How ya doin'?"

"State your business."

"I wanna come in."

"Course you do," I said. "Who doesn't? Beat it, beastly."

"I got a proposition," she said.

"We already heard from your boss. We're not interested in being Wolf Gangers."

"Neither am I," she answered. "It turned out to be the wimpiest club since the Camp Fire Girls."

Now she had my attention. And Ling's, and Cecil's, as the two of them slithered their way out of the car and toward the door, where I was.

"No kidding?" I said, but then I didn't want to sound too excited. "Well, right, naturally. I could have told you that a long time ago. So, tell me, what is it you do want here, Nessy?"

"I wanna be a He-Man," she said.

Now, most times, a guy can keep his cool no matter what a person says to him. Then, there are other times . . .

"You wanna be a *what*? A what? A what?" I babbled. I turned to Ling. "Ling, what did she say? She wants to be a *what*? Did she say what I thought she—"

"A what?" Ling babbled right back. "I think she said . . . no, I have to be wrong. I know she didn't say . . ."

Nessy, from out on the sidewalk, was laughing raucously.

"Cecil?" I said, obviously desperate. "Cecil, buddy, did she say that she wants . . . in my precious He-Man . . . ?"

Cecil cupped his hands over his ears, in case she said it again.

She said it again.

"I mean it. I want to be in your club. Don't be afraid. Think about it for a minute. I will be the best new member you ever had. One, I could whip all you guys *and* all the Wolf Gangers, at the same time, blindfolded, with a dress on. Two, you're down to practically no members left as it is, and you'll have to take my word for it—there ain't no line gathering behind me out here to sign up. And three, I guarantee you I hate those other guys even more than you do, and we all know the kind of stuff I'm capable of once I get heated up about something."

Ling quietly groaned his agreement and rubbed his big round belly. She once gave him such a vicious finger-poking in the stomach that his mom took him to the hospital to see if his appendix had burst.

"So," she said, "what do ya say?"

What do I say? This was the He-Man Women

Haters Club, for crying out loud. Sure, we didn't have the sign hanging outside yet, but still, everybody knew. . . .

"Ah, Vanessa," I said carefully. "You know, there's this problem. After all, you *are* a girl . . . I mean . . . right?"

She paused, then answered with an offended tone.

"Not hardly, I ain't," she said.

There was—for the first time in a long time—agreement among the He-Man ranks. She wasn't hardly a Women as far as we three were concerned.

"I don't know, Nessy. We have to huddle on this one."

She was growing impatient with us. "Oh jeez, ya big buncha babies. So go on and huddle already, but be quick about it."

We huddled. She interrupted. "But don't forget. If I ain't a member of the club, then I'm a dismember."

I do believe she could hear the triple gulp all the way out there on the sidewalk. That would explain her laughter, anyway.

I surveyed my men.

"What do I think?" Cecil repeated. "I think I

ain't never met such a skeery little bit of a thing in my life. I think if we let her in, I won't never have a minute's peace inside this garage again."

"And if we don't," Ling added, "you won't have a minute's peace *outside* it."

"Good point," Cecil said.

"Oh, this is pretty," I said. "The two of you sure are a recruiting poster for the club. Why don't we just sign up every kid who makes you nervous, huh? We'd have to find a bigger garage to hold them all, but at least we'd never be lonely."

"Hey, good one, Johnny," Ness called from way yonder.

"All right," I said. "She even has ears like a golden retriever."

"More like a bat," she said.

The sad part was, it was so plain to see that Vanessa was—after myself, of course—the He-Manliest recruit we'd ever had. But that wasn't the issue here, was it?

"We have discussed it," I announced, even though it wasn't much of a discussion and Vanessa heard every word. "And we're not interested. We're not afraid of you, ya gargoyle, and we can't see what good you could do us anyway."

She was totally cool and unflustered, just like

I like to be. "What good I could do you?" she responded as the three of us headed back to the safety of the Lincoln, where we would probably spend the rest of our days now. "Well, I figure, since I am still officially a Wolf Ganger, and since nobody knows I'm here . . . I might make one mighty mighty double agent . . ."

I stopped in my tracks. The other boys kept walking, because they don't have my *vision*.

". . . and I might very well be the exact thing someone might need, if they were interested in bringing the Wolf Gang and its leader . . ."

"To his *kneeeeeees* . . ." I hooted as I spun and raced to unbolt the door.

"Welcome aboard, He-Man Vanessa," I said, shaking her scaly little hand. But before I let her in, I stopped her. "One question first: Why?"

She shook her head, tightened her lips so hard her mouth looked like a white Life Saver.

"If you could see what those . . . *girls* . . . have done to my little Jerome . . ."

There was blood in Vanessa's eyes. Now, more than ever, I was glad I was not one of those . . . *girls*.

6
Bring 'em Back Alive . . .
or Not

Who'd have believed it?

We went from being a nearly dead-in-the-water, over-the-hill, lifeless has-been outfit to being a mean and motivated crack operation overnight.

And it was all because of a girl.

Well, not a girl, exactly, but Vanessa, which was close enough.

"You, chubby," she barked at Ling. "You're gonna have to stay on the outside watching from the street because there ain't no crevices with the capacity to hide you."

He saluted her. No lie, Ling saluted her, and accepted his assignment as if it came straight down from his hero, General Patton himself.

She was very hard to not listen to.

"You, beanpole." That would be Cecil. "Lemme see you imitate a coatrack."

We waited and watched.

"Excellent," Nessy said. "That'll work fine."

Cecil raised his hand. "But I ain't done nothin' yet. I was just thinkin' 'bout it. . . ."

"Great," she said. "When the time comes, you just think, and you'll look like a coatrack.

"You." Me.

"Wait right there," I said. "Don't think you're going to start bossing me. Here in *my* club—"

"Course not," she replied. "Wouldn't think of it."

She stopped, and waited.

"All right then," I said after a respectful waiting period. "So what do I do, Ness?"

When we got to the shop, the first order of business was to survey the situation from the outside. The four of us crouched down behind a line of parked cars. It was a little difficult to see and not be seen. But even through the windows of the car that hid us, and the plate glass of Yvette's big showy storefront, what we saw was sickening.

There he was, our Jerome, back in the same spot where we had left him that fateful day. He was getting his nails done again, right up there in the front window for the whole world to see.

"How often does he get his nails done?" I asked.

"Every day that he's here," she said. "Can you believe this? Look at him, Johnny. Will ya look what they've done to our boy?"

He was "our boy." Mine, because he was an original He-Man. Nessy's, because she had long held a dream of carrying Jerome off on her back to live in her cave.

"He was such a . . . *man* before they got ahold of him."

Even I wouldn't go that far. But I got the point.

"He certainly is a mess," I agreed. Even through all the glass and across that distance, you could see the sheen coming off the hand that had already been polished. It was like he was wearing a set of tiny white Christmas lights on his fingertips.

"That looks a little different to me," I said. "It doesn't look like before, when he was just getting his nails buffed up like a shoeshine. There's . . . something in there."

"It's called a French manicure," she said with so much disgust and anger, I thought she'd tear the side panel right off the car. "They give him the high shine, then paint just the very tips with little half-moons of white polish."

"Oh my god," Ling said. I was thinking it too, but could not form words at that point.

Nessy was staring flames in the direction of the manicurist. "She holds his hand way longer than she needs to. If she don't let go of him in the next two minutes, I'm gonna be her next customer. I'll let her buff my knuckles with her forehead."

My, the new recruit was fitting in nicely.

"All right, let's move in," Vanessa said. "This is our moment. The only ones in the shop this early are Jerome and his personal stylist there, so we need to set up now."

We left Ling there skulking around out front, while Cecil, Vanessa, and I went around to the infamous aquamarine door. Once inside, Vanessa manhandled Cecil up against the wall, stripped the real coatrack of all its sweaters, pink rubber raincoats, and umbrellas, and piled them high on Cecil. She then shoved him behind the vinyl sofa/hair dryer station. He looked no different from the real rack, which she laid on the floor.

"Cecil, you're a natural, man. You ever done any acting before?" I asked.

"You can tell, huh? Truth is, I played Winnie-the-Pooh in the local theater one time. Remember the time ol' Pooh got hisself stuck in rabbit's hole 'cause he was eatin' way too much honey? . . ." Cecil laughed at the memory. "Course, I only played the back-end part of Pooh, for the scenes when Tigger an' them guys were tryin' to get his little bear butt out of—"

"Act like a coatrack!" Nessy snapped. It would take her longer than most to get used to He-Man Cecil.

Myself, I got the prime spot. It was a small, secret passageway that ran the length of the building, behind the salon's wall. When I slipped myself into the space, I practically got pinned between the cinder-block exterior wall behind me and the two-by-four studs that framed the interior one. I felt like a rat, squiggling around inside the hidden dark places where nobody else would go.

"So what am I supposed to do from in here?" I asked as Nessy pointed me into position.

"Keep going, keep going," she said.

After I'd slid about ten feet in, I reached the spot. Right there in front of my face, the whole front room of Yvette's Hair-Nails-Aromatherapy salon opened up, like a wide-screen TV program. I was behind the big mirror where the person getting clipped stares at herself. It wasn't exactly a two-way mirror, but at that range it was awfully close.

"Isn't it illegal or something," I asked, "to have spying equipment in a place of business?"

She shrugged. "It might be illegal, but it sure is a lot of fun. You ever watch someone closely when they're watching themselves closely?"

I don't even like to watch myself closely.

"No," I said.

"Have fun," Ness said, and disappeared.

The first subject I got to test it out on was, of course, Jerome. Fresh from his French fry finger festival, he walked directly to the hair chair right in front of me. There was nobody there to wait on him, so he killed time.

I barely recognized the creature before me. He wore these baggy wool pants that came to a tight tapered peg at the ankle. He wore a crisply pressed sky-blue shirt with a foolish little polo player whacking its way across the pocket. His shirt was neatly and permanently tucked in at the waist (which is significant because the waist of Jerome's pants used to be yanked up so high you wouldn't have been able to *see* the little polo man). Suspenders kept the pants in place.

Suspenders, for crying out loud.

"Dink," I muttered before I could clap a hand over my mouth.

Jerome looked up at the sound of my voice. He stared straight at me, as if looking for me. I stopped breathing. He stared closer. He got up out of the chair and took the three steps to where he was nose up with the mirror. And with me.

A look of recognition came over his face, and a knowing smile. I knew I was cooked.

Then he smiled broadly, licked his teeth. Took a step back. Fingered an early-stage pimple on his chin, pointed at his reflection, and winked.

At himself.

The risk of giving away my position was the only thing that kept me from retching right there.

As Jerome remounted his throne, Yvette and her rotten little daughter Monica strolled in.

"Ah, all ready for another hard day in the salt mines, eh, Jerome?" Yvette joked.

"Oh, no salt," he answered. "You know it dries my skin out something awful."

I began a silent dialogue with Jerome.

"I'm gonna do something awful to your skin, boy. . . ."

Jerome patted the very top of his new mountain of sprayed, bent, folded, and pompadoured country-singer hair. "Do you have time to just clip the sideburns, Yvette?"

"Sideburns?" I croaked. "You pimple-faced, white-washed, snotty-nosed . . . you couldn't grow even *one* decent sideburn if we fertilized your face *and* left you out in the sun all summer."

"Sure," Yvette said. "We've got time."

As the trimming began, Monica approached. "Ma, not again. Tell me you're not going to waste another day working on Conway Twit over here."

"Never mind about him, Mon, just go over there and make sure the aromas are all filled."

"I always *wanted* a little sister anyway," Monica groused as she left.

Good one, Monica. You're still a beast, though.

Vanessa, cool as could be, came marching in from the back room. She walked right up and stood next to the "client," the two of them now staring straight ahead to where I was. Vanessa looked so unnatural and guilty, I wouldn't have been surprised if her first words were, "Morning, everybody, I'm a dirty rotten double agent, did I tell you that?"

"Can I do something for you, Ness?" Yvette asked her.

"Oh, um, no. My hair's perfect, thanks."

Sure, if you think steel wool is perfect.

"Vanessa, you're blocking my light," Jerome said in a shockingly bold and un-Jerome-y move.

"There are fifty million lights in this place, Jerome," she answered.

"Yes, but that one back there makes me look more like I have lips."

Vanessa stared triple-depth into me. "See," she said, pointing at Jerome.

"See what?" Jerome asked.

Nessy was already heading back to the store-room. "See what a simp a boy turns into if he doesn't have four other boys around him at all times."

Everyone in the place said, "Huh?" but she just slammed the door behind her.

"Come on, Yvette," Jerome said as his clipping was ending. "When do I get to work on some-body?"

Excuse me?

"We'll see."

"Oh, please? You keep saying I'll get to cut some hair, but then you don't let me."

Come again? This couldn't be. This could not be. No, not even a *former* He-Man can work in a beauty parlor. This was just getting to be more than I could bear.

I slithered my way along the wall, back toward the storeroom. I peeked in to find the coast still clear. Cecil was doing an amazing coatrack, super-human. Vanessa was working away like a squirrel

49

(or an employee on the last day of a job) yanking Girl Scout cookies out of their boxes and stashing the inner packages into her pockets.

"Hey, Cecil," I said. "This has reached crisis stage. We have to do something, and we have to do it now. There is absolutely nothing left of the Jerome we knew, and if we don't help him immediately, I don't know if we'll be able to bring him all the way back."

"Told ya," Vanessa said, hiding an extra few cookies in her mouth.

Cecil, rigid as an oak, had not responded. He was still in character.

"Cecil," I said, "you can stop being a coatrack for a minute. I have to talk to you."

Nothing.

"Cecil," I said, nudging the great stack of jackets in roughly the spot where Cecil's ribs would be.

"Wha—?" he responded, making the unmistakable snort noise of a person being startled awake.

"How can you sleep standing up?" I asked.

"Horses do it all the time," he answered. "It was so dark and warm . . ."

"How long before Wolf gets here?" I asked Ness.

"Not long. You wanna do something, you have

50

to do it soon. He might be out there right now, in fact."

I jumped.

Not that I was afraid of him or anything. It was just, well, anyway . . .

"I better go check," I said, then started up the wall alley again. I was halfway there when I heard the door from the shop to the back room open and Jerome's sappy voice yipping.

"It's my chance, it's my chance," he said excitedly. "Yvette said I could do it, and Wolf said he'd let me cut his hair."

Holy—

I scurried the last few feet to see Wolf being lifted out of his wheelchair by Ling's sister, Rock, Yvette, and Monica, and placed ever so gently in the chair. I quickly made my way back toward Vanessa.

"See, this is the difference," Jerome said as he frantically rummaged through shelves and boxes in the storeroom. "This is what leadership and loyalty are all about. You think Johnny Nosehair would ever let me work on him? Right."

Keep digging there, Jerome.

"What are you looking for?" Vanessa asked.

"Yvette said I have to wear a white smock like

everybody else if I'm going to work on anybody. She said it's in here, but I can't find it. I can't find it. I can't—"

"Oh, that," Ness said with an exaggerated nod. She glanced over to where I was peeking out of my hole and gave me the high sign. "I know where that is. It's right there on the coatrack."

Yesssss! Vanessa, rookie of the year in the He-Man league.

"Where?" Jerome said suspiciously. "I don't see any smock there. I just see coats."

"Right there," she said. "Under the rain slicker."

As Jerome made his way to the slicker, I inched up, ready to pounce. Cecil hovered, looming high above our once and future comrade, waiting.

Jerome snatched away the slicker, revealing no smock.

"See?" he said. "I knew it wasn't there."

Come on, Cecil, come on.

"It's in there," Vanessa prodded. "Keep poking around."

So he did. He prodded around so thoroughly, Cecil wouldn't need a physical for another year. But Cecil did not react.

He was asleep again.

Vanessa stomped over to the couch, stood on

the back of it between two hair dryer helmets, and started slapping the coatrack on the side of the head. "Keep . . . looking . . . in . . . here," she said, slapping with each word.

The coatrack stirred. Jerome dug deeper. The coatrack started giggling.

I heard Monica on the other side of the door. "All right, all right, I'll check. Maybe Precious got lost. . . ."

I jumped out of hiding. "Grab him, Cecil," I said. And Cecil did.

"Jerome, my mom wants to know what's taking so—" Monica stopped and stared as I grabbed Jerome from the back, and the mound of jackets was wrapping him up from the front, and Vanessa stood munching cookies. I looked to see what Monica was going to do, and she made a motion to go back and tell her mother but then stopped, closed the door, and approached Nessy.

"Are those the butter cookies," Monica asked casually, "or the sugar cookies?"

Under one particularly heavy wool sweater Jerome was muffling, "Help. Help me, please . . ."

"Oh, I can't eat more than a couple of the sugar cookies or I feel nauseous," Vanessa said, and the two of them slid down into side-by-side positions on the couch. When Jerome's struggling got more serious and more pathetic, they pulled the hanging hair dryer helmets down over their heads.

"Good," Monica said, taking a cookie. "I like the butter ones better too."

As Cecil and I wrestled the squirming Jerome out the aquamarine door, Monica called to us, "Try to keep a better eye on him next time, wouldja? We don't want him running away and showing up here again."

7
Get with the Program

"Stop it, you're messing up my hair," said Jerome, still a-kickin' and a-whinin' when we brought him in.

When the door to Lars's garage was shut and bolted behind us, we finally let him go.

"Welcome home, Jerome," I said.

"Welcome to jail, you criminal moron," he responded.

"Ling," I commanded, "sit on him."

Good soldier that he is, Ling grabbed Jerome, apologized, then squashed him on the cold concrete floor.

"Now, criminal moron?" Ling asked, as if they were carrying on a casual, friendly conversation. "Does that mean he's so dumb it's a crime, or does it mean he's unintelligent and just also happens to be a person who commits crimes?"

"I have not committed any crimes," I insisted.

"Kidnapping is a crime," Jerome wheezed from under the bulk of Ling.

"You are not kidnapped," I said. "You're rescued."

"Oh god," said Cecil. "What we done? Are we goin' ta jail? I heard about jail from my uncle Jack, and I don't think I'm gon' like it much."

"Too bad," Jerome said, trying bravely to fix his hair with his one free hand, without a mirror. "Because you are going to prison once I get out of here."

I was not nervous. "We are not going to jail."

"Because you are *not* getting out," Ling added.

"No, that's not it," I assured them all. "It's because, once we deprogram you, you are not only not going to put us in jail, you are going to thank us for saving you." I motioned to Ling to let the prisoner up. He did, and Jerome creakily got to his feet and dusted off.

Just then Lars came running down from his office. "What is *he* doing back here? I thought we lost this bad penny. And *what* happened to him? Boy, Jerome, you was a sorry enough sight before, but now you look like a little Ken doll, only wimpier."

"I missed you too, Lars," Jerome said.

"No time for this, guys," Ling cut in. "We've got deprogramming to do." Ling was really warming up to this now.

"Lemme in. Lemme in." It was Vanessa. She must have thought by then that that was the password, because that's what she did instead of knocking.

"How'd it go back there?" I asked as she strolled in.

"Cool. I told Wolfgang that Jerome ran off, and he said, 'Good. That's how you can tell Jerome's a member of a club, 'cause he keeps on quitting it.'"

I laughed, from experience. Wolf was right on that one.

"Wolf said that about me?" Jerome was wounded.

"Hey there, Jerome," Nessy said proudly. "Nice to see you again."

"Is it, like, your life's mission to haunt my every conscious moment?" he asked her.

"As a matter of fact, it is," she answered with a smile.

He's lucky, I thought. At least she limits it to his conscious moments. My most recent Monica haunt had come just the night before, when I dreamed an entire scene from *King Kong* in which Monica was climbing the outside of the Empire State Building with me in her fist. When she got to the top, she celebrated by kissing me with big blue blubber lips the size of water beds.

We hauled Jerome through the garage and into the Lincoln. Inside, it was warm and cozy and familiar. I sat in the driver's seat, of course. Jerome got shotgun. Ling and Cecil sat in back, flanking Nessy.

"Nice wheels," she said, running her mitts up and down all over the upholstery.

"Don't do that," I said. She stopped, but Jerome wouldn't take his eyes off her.

"See, doesn't this feel nice, like old times?" I said to Jerome.

"Make up your mind, Steven," he snipped. "Does it feel nice, or does it feel like old times?"

"Har-har. But admit it, doesn't it feel better? Doesn't it feel right, here with your old friends?"

"Well . . . I do like the car . . . and I suppose you guys . . ."

I could feel him coming back to us. No way he could resist the total He-Man experience.

". . . but you don't know . . . the rich feel of mousse foaming through your fingers . . . the smell of aerosol all day long . . ."

"That explains it," I said. "Aerosol spray's making you daffy."

"No, it doesn't, Steven. I'm serious. If you guys would only give me a chance . . . if you would open yourselves up to the experience of a higher level of personal hygiene . . ."

"Not us, none of that, no hygiene," Cecil said.

"Never mind all that," I said. "Think about it this way: Wolfgang—who you fear—was here, and now he's there; Monica and the Scouts—who you also fear—are over there as well. Remember the savage snowballing incident, when they left you for practically dead before I rescued you and took you in here?"

Good play, Steve-o. Tap his scarediness *and* his sappiness.

Jerome turned all red, and growled.

"Right," I pointed out. "And now, you are in a *club* with them?"

"Ya," Jerome said, digging in, "well, you might be right about that other stuff, but I was *this* close to being an honest-to-goodness hairstylist. Laugh if you want to—"

I wanted to, but was sure it wouldn't help things.

"Har-har-har . . ." Cecil had no such reservations.

"But at least I have a dream. You fix cars and count chest hairs, Steven. Ling, you have a dream filled with bazookas and aircraft carriers and you can fly. Cecil, you have a dream too, probably. I'm sure your dream is like, a dial tone or something, but it is your dream. Me, I'm a creative artist. I want to make the world more beautiful, one unsightly person at a time. Ness the Mess . . ."

My, the prisoner was feeling bold. Everyone knows that nickname, but people do not often call Vanessa Ness the Mess and walk away from the conversation under their own power.

"Nessy, you have a dream too, I bet."

Nessy put on a very serious face, and nodded. She leaned over the front seat to tell her dream to Jerome privately.

"Oh my god!" Jerome shrieked, pulling away from her. "Well, your dream will *not* be coming true anytime soon, I can assure you."

Meanwhile, the He-Man leader was thinking on his feet.

"Jerome, we are aware that that's what you want

to do. Word's out on the street, buddy."

"It is?"

"Sure. And that's why we came to get you. We said to ourselves, you know, things just ain't right here without Jerome. And then to think he's over there, slaving and cutting hair for people . . . who don't appreciate him . . ."

"You know, you're right about that, they don't really appreciate me there."

". . . people who threw snowballs at him . . ."

"You think I forget? You think I ever close my eyes on them? Winter's coming up too, don't forget. Who knows when they'll get the snow-balling urge again."

". . . people who have no respect for his *He-Man* qualities . . ."

"Now, that's not true, Steven. No, they can see my He-Man—"

"Wake up and smell the aromatherapy, Jerome," I said. "Didn't you wonder why you were the only He-Man Wolfgang stole for his new club? Did you not notice that you were the only *Man* in the whole place besides him?"

"Well, I did wonder. . . ."

"It's because Wolfgang doesn't like guys at all!"

61

I announced it as if I had exposed Wolfgang as a Nazi war criminal.

"He only likes *women*, and mousy little guys who are no threat to him. That is why—you will recall—Wolfgang had nothing but problems with ol' Johnny Chesthair. Too much man, plain and simple."

"He said that? About me?" Jerome was outraged.

"Ya . . ." I fudged, ". . . at some point, I'm sure he has . . . said more or less what I just said. And to think you were over there working for that rat when we, your old buddies, were here, so badly in need of somebody to cut some hair right here."

"What?" he said. "No. You're pulling my leg."

"We don't pull nothing here, Jerome, you know that. We need you. I mean just this morning Cecil was moaning that if he didn't get somebody to give him a trim, he wouldn't be able to leave the house pretty soon." I leaned in close to Jerome, to make sure I nailed the target straight on. "'Cause you know, the poor kid's got no money to pay for something like that."

"How come I don't remember sayin' nothin' like that?" Cecil asked nervously.

"Ah, because you were sleeping. It was when you were sleeping."

"Oh. Well, anyways, if I said it then I musta meant it, huh? And if I say somethin', I make good on it. Everybody knows that about me."

Jerome was staring at Cecil hard now. "You know, I didn't want to say anything before, but you are looking a little like a sheepdog there, Cecil."

"Heck, let's fix me, then," he said.

I didn't want to lose the momentum. I threw open the car door. "Yo, Lars, you have anything like scissors back there?"

Lars dug into his great big Snap-on toolbox. "I got some long-nose wire cutters."

"Fine," I said. It wasn't *my* hair, after all.

"They're a little greasy, but they're plenty sharp."

"That'll do," I said.

I turned to Jerome and offered him my hand. "Back in the fold, *He-Man*?" I asked.

"I have missed that," he said, shaking my hand. "Being called a Wolf Ganger made me feel a little dirty."

"Cool. Just one thing."

"Name it."

"Barber shop."

"Barber shop?"

63

"Barber shop, right. Where we set you up, where you're going to do your business. It'll be called a barber shop. Not, you know, not a salon or nothing like that. That just wouldn't work for us. All right?"

8
Cecil's Dream

The next day when I got to the club, Jerome was already open for business. Way open.

We had an old velour bucket seat from a '67 Mustang that had been kicking around the shop forever. Jerome was using that as his barber chair, pumping it up and down with a hydraulic jack. Ling was sitting in the waiting area, browsing a *Wolverine* comic, and Cecil was up there in the chair.

"Still?" I asked Cecil.

"No, again," answered Jerome. "We had more work to do, so we continued this morning."

Cecil was reclined all the way back, while Jerome fooled around combing the mop of hair forward, back, sideways, and then scrambling it all up to start over.

"And I do so have a dream," Cecil blurted. Poor guy, he must have been nursing this all the way since yesterday, which is a very long time for Cecil to hold a thought. "I have a dream, just like the rest of y'all, and it don't sound like no dial tone, neither."

"Hey, I'm sorry about that, Cecil. I was just mad."

"Ya, well, my dream is . . . I want to fix televisions."

There was a pretty large silence in the crowd. Nobody wanted to laugh, what with Cecil being hurt enough already, but it was hard to know what to say to make him feel good, either.

But after all, I was the leader around here.

"That's . . . ah, that's nice, Cecil. But how come you want—"

He was gritting his teeth. He was truly angry here, something I'd never seen from him before.

"Because," he said. "Because that's my dream and it's a good dream. It ain't like your dream, Steven, which is to make people obey you, or your dream, Jerome, which is to make people not hurt your eyes, or your dream, Ling, which is to make people blow up. I have this dream all the time and it is just to make folks happy. And I don't know every darn thing but I know that television makes folks happy. I fix their broke televisions and they're happy and then I'm happy."

I couldn't even think of a joke for that. He had us all whipped, the big dumb thing. I don't think any of the other dreams ended with the dreamer being happy.

"Good dream, Cecil," I said, and I determined right then that I was going to modify my dream. I was going to stop focusing on negative, hateful, stupid stuff, and I was going to be happy.

Bang-bang-bang-bang-bang.

Someone was at the door. Me and my new attitude went to answer it.

"Open up. It's me, Rock, and I wanna come in."

"Get outta here, ya big rotten *girl*," I screamed.

Good-bye new attitude. Glad I got that out of my system.

"It's okay" came a second voice, Nessy's. "She's with me."

"So why does that make it okay?" Jerome said, leaving Cecil stranded in the chair. He turned to me. "Now's your chance, Steven. Don't let her in."

Cecil ran right up beside him, to address the other one. "Go home, Rock," he yelled. "You don't belong here."

"I wanna be a He-Man too," she said. "Like Vanessa."

Ling turned to me. "Now see what you did? You let down your guard for the first one, now they're all coming in under the door like roaches."

"Calm down now," I said. "It's not such a—"

My men ignored me. "Go away!" they both screamed together, but at their separate targets.

"Come on," Rock reasoned. "We want to be on your side. Wolfgang's a rat, and we want to help you whip him."

Hello, personal quest.

"Maybe we should consider—" I tried.

"Get out!" Ling screamed. I didn't recall ever hearing Ling scream before. "Get out of here, Rock, or I'll . . ."

All she did from her side of the door was laugh mercilessly.

"I'll . . . tell Mom."

Now Rock and Vanessa were both laughing.

"That didn't help," I said. "Listen, girls. We have standards, you know. We can't just let you in because you feel like—"

"I'll whip any He-Man in the joint," Rock insisted. "You prove me wrong—heh-heh—and I'll go away. If I win, I'll just be the toughest He-Man in the place, at your service. You can't lose, in a way."

I turned to Ling. "Well, she's your sister," I said.

Ling shrugged, backing away from the door as if

it couldn't protect him from her.

"So I guess that means you're not taking her on," I said to Ling. I turned to Jerome.

"You're joking, right?" he asked. "I wouldn't even fight their mom."

Since Cecil was fully reclined in the barber chair off in TV-repairman heaven, snoring like a tractor engine, we were left once more with the last line of defense.

Johnny on the spot again.

"Come on, ya big chickens," Rock called, kicking the metal door and making a thunderstormlike racket.

"Ya, ya big babies," Ness added, kicking right along.

Slowly—but with dignity—I began sliding the dead bolt open. There were only bad things on the other side of that door, but there are times when a man's got no choice. . . .

"Hey!" my uncle Lars screamed, storming out of his office. "Who is out here banging on my doors, making all that noise, screaming? . . . This is a place of business. . . . You know how much a door like that costs? . . . I'll teach ya, ya rotten punks. . . ."

"Ah, Lars . . ." I said weakly as the bolt un-latched.

Like a jack-in-the-box, Rock exploded through

the door as soon as it was unlocked. She blasted right past me and met up with . . . shocked Uncle Lars.

"Holy—" he yelped.

There was an audible crash of bones when Lars and Rock locked. She put this great two-handed claw-hold on both of his shoulders and drove him backward, all the way across the garage. The crowd followed the action, like it was a normal street brawl.

"Oh my god, oh my god, oh my god," Lars moaned as she tossed him around.

Jerome laughed. "Hey, he sounds like me."

"Who are you? *What* are you? What are you *doing*?" Lars was understandably a little lost.

"I am Rock. I am your worst nightmare. And I am beating you up," she answered helpfully before hip-rolling him to the floor.

She dropped on top of him, with her elbow digging into his ribs.

"*Oooofff!*" The door slammed behind us, with the rush of wind that escaped poor Lars.

"I love it when she makes them go *oooofff*," Nessy said.

Rock stood up. Lars did not. Rock dropped down again. Same elbow, same ribs.

70

"Oooofff!"

Rock stood up. Lars did not.

She came over to the crowd and shook my hand without my even offering it. "So then, anybody else?"

"Welcome aboard," I said. Then I went over to where Lars was struggling to his feet. "You okay?" I asked, taking him by the arm.

"Sure I am. Fine. Just, you know, had one of my epileptic seizures. Happens all the time. Nobody was watching, was they?"

"No," I assured him.

"Good," he said. "Because, of course, they're a lot worse to look at than they actually are."

"Sure," I said. "I know. Listen, you want a haircut? How would you like a nice haircut?"

"That'd be nice, thanks," he said.

I signaled Jerome, who stared at Lars. "He better have his own comb," Jerome said. "Because I am not running mine through that. No way."

9
Steven's Dream

Now it all made sense to me. Like a vision, like a dream, like a sign from above, my purpose was clear.

Steal every last one of renegade He-Man Wolfgang's recruits. Break him. Stomp him. Show him who's boss once and for all. Maybe, just maybe then, when he comes home, crawling on his hands . . . his hands and hips, or whatever . . . maybe then when he's left the dark side of the force and begs me to bring him back . . .

I will say no.

I brought back Jerome. I lured Nessy. I got Rock. This was all so predictable. Of course the world would wind up beating a path to the He-Man door.

And so what if our two roughest He-Men— besides me—happened to be girls? They weren't the girly kind of girls, that's for sure. And wasn't this the 1990s, after all? Sure, we're cool.

"I'm still the boss, remember," I said to the two new ones at indoctrination.

"Ya, sure," they snickered.

That makes me so mad.

"Hey!" I said, yanking up my shirt to give them a good fright. "You see these?"

We all know what I was pointing at.

"Take a good look. He who wears the chesthairs calls the shots in this club."

"My," Rock said, acting impressed. "He seems to be spraying a lot of testosterone today."

Cecil was walking by. "Testost . . . what is that? What's he spraying?" He looked me up and down nervously as he asked.

Rock laughed. "It's a chemical, Abner. It's what makes men all . . . *manly*."

You could not have missed Rock's sarcasm from across town.

Cecil missed it.

"Coach," he said to me, "I make a recommendation that we get us some of this stuff. Sounds like just the thing we should have in stock. Where can we get it? Does it come in cans or what?"

The girls were laughing it up.

"Don't worry, Cecil," I assured him. "We've got

plenty." I turned to Ness and Rock. "You two. I have made an executive decision—which I do all the time, as a matter of fact. I am signing you up as Junior . . . ah . . . Associate Level . . . Secondary members of the club. Also called GALS—"

"What?" Rock said.

"It's a temporary, provisional thing. Only until we have been satisfied as to your loyalty and trustworthiness."

Rock ran over and grabbed her brother by the collar and pulled him right up out of the barber chair.

"Hey, I'm nowhere near finished with that," Jerome protested.

And he sure wasn't. Ling looked like a half-eaten bowl of spaghetti.

"Do you mean to tell me," Rock demanded, "that this worm had to go through your stupid GALS program?"

"No, he did not."

"Then why do I?"

"Because . . . well, come on, you know why."

"No, spell it out for me."

"Because girls are not as trustworthy as boys."

Rock was actually restrained by Nessy from going after me. Nessy got up on her toes and

74

whispered in her ear. Rock smiled and nodded. "Oh ya, you did tell me he'd do a lot of stupid things before he learned not to be afraid of us."

"I am not—"

"Fine, fine," Rock said. "We're GALS. Let's get on with destroying Wolfgang."

Ah, mutual ground.

"Good," I said, rubbing my hands together. "But first, tell me your name. I know it's not Rock, and if we're going to be working together . . ."

"My real name is Duke."

"Fine then, Rock, here's what I need to ask you: Do you, in fact, hate women?"

This was the test. They couldn't possibly fake this. If they said yes, then they had to mean it. If they said no, they were out.

"Yes," Rock said confidently.

Well, that was a surprise.

"But we don't hate all of 'em," Nessy squawked. "Let's get that straight right now. I hate the one that held Jerome's hand all day long."

"And I hate *Monica*," Rock growled with a most impressive bone-deep hatred.

"It's not necessarily the quantity but the quality of your Women-Hating that matters here. And

Rocko, you picked a good one." I walked over and we exchanged high fives. When Rock's big meaty hand slapped my normal one, my whole arm bent backward—and not at the elbow, either; it was the forearm bone that bowed.

"Ouch," I said. "So what is it? What makes you hate her so much?" I walked them over to the Lincoln and leaned comfortably against the fender, preparing to enjoy a delightful story.

They told it as a team.

Nessy: "It's him, really, Wolf-face."

Rock: "Him *and* her."

N: "Right. See, he was supposed to be hers—Rock's, that is."

R: "He was. He was mine. And I fell for it. It was always, 'Yo, Rock, pick me up. Rock, scratch my back where I can't reach. Rock, can you wheel me to the store for a jerky stick, and by the way, could ya pay for it too? Yo, Rock, I'm bored, could ya break another brick with your head?'"

Oh yes, that sounded like our Wolfgang.

R: "I'd give him a jerky stick . . . and all the while . . ."

N: "The whole time . . ."

They were getting all frothed up. I wished I had some popcorn and a Coke.

R: "He was just slobbering over *her*. The little mouse. Then, the day I walked in and he was giving her rides around the shop in his chair . . . *grrrrrrr.*"

Pang!

Whoa. Where did that come from? I must have forgotten to eat breakfast this morning.

"And remember?" Ness added. "When we came in and found him shampooing her hair? . . ."

Pang! Zip! Zing!

What was going on here? My stomach had no business, no business at all, doing these things to me. What could I possibly have cared what the two of them did in the privacy of their own . . . sick, demented, disgusting little club?

"That's it," I announced. "He's out of business. We are going to put his club into the ground no matter what it takes."

"It wouldn't take much," Rock said. "The other girls are pretty well sick of him too. All you have to do is give me the okay, and I can have them all over here with us in fifteen minutes."

It was evidence of how crazy I'd gotten that I didn't even hesitate before saying, "Go get 'em!"

My original, male, club brothers had been

listening in closer and closer as this conversation grew, and at this point rushed in.

"Are you *nuts*?" they all yelled together, as if they'd been rehearsing.

They just didn't understand, which was okay because leadership was my job.

"No," I said. "I am not crazy; I have a vision."

"Crazy people have visions all the time," Jerome answered. "Isn't that right, Cecil?"

"Huh?" Cecil asked.

I sent the GALS out to do their job and proceeded to gather my men into the car to explain the plan. "We have to do some dirty work here, guys. Because we have a mission. Once Wolf is destroyed, we will deal with the fallout here, but at least then we won't be fighting a war on two fronts." I ended with a big wink.

Ling winked back. It didn't matter what I said, as long as I talked in military terms, he was with me.

Cecil winked back. He hadn't the slightest idea what I said, but he didn't like to be left behind.

Jerome stared at me hard, a fatherly glare like the He-Man Club founder that he was. "Steven," he said sternly, "I still say you're nuts. But as an initiation, every new member has to let me cut his or her hair. And if they don't like what they get, they're out."

Every man has his mission. And his price.

10
The Sweet Smell of Victory

The bright side: It turned out to be fortunate that Wolfgang was the kind of guy nobody wanted to tell when they quit his club. I was loaded with double agents. So just like that, my club was filled with all the members we'd stolen from Wolfgang's club.

The dark side: My club was filled with all the members we'd stolen from Wolfgang's club.

We didn't know what to do with ourselves. The He-Man Women Haters was never built to be this big. It was never built—duh, no kidding, Steve-o—to have women there either. I tried to spend more time inside the car, but one of the new recruits had hung a rosewood air freshener inside, and even after I'd removed—and stomped—the thing, the scent was there to stay. The whole experience of the car was perverted now.

And if I went under the hood, or under the

chassis on the creeper, Rock would already be under there, fixing something, having the time of her life.

Jerome wouldn't stop lodging official complaints that Vanessa had once again picked him up and squeezed him.

Cecil did nothing anymore but lie on the floor on an old piece of carpet he'd found, occasionally scratching behind one ear with his foot.

Ling was into one more of his full-blown transformations, walking around in a velvet smoking jacket and having Jerome give him a new hairstyle every day. Hairstyles had replaced hats as Ling's disguise of choice.

"The pressure is killing me," Jerome said of the demand.

My uncle Lars refused to come out of his office from the time the girls arrived to the time they left for supper. He did all his work at night. Some days he didn't even show, and I had to open the garage and receive customers myself.

Finally, I just had to get out. I had soundly whipped the enemy, but found it to be a hollow victory.

The only pleasure left was to go over there and revel in it.

I knew when to get there, and where to go, so by the time Wolfgang did show up, I was already in the wall, watching Yvette and the manicurist do their boring, girly business. I was happy to see Wolfgang show up because I figured at least now it would be interesting.

I had no idea.

The first thing I saw was Wolf—the once-mighty, rotten, slick, sinister Wolf—roll up to Yvette and ask her if he could get her some tea.

"No thank you," she said, continuing to clip without even looking at him.

"Really?" he asked. "I picked up some Earl Grey on the way over today because I knew—"

"Wolfgang," Yvette snapped at him. Then she composed herself, took a deep breath, and spoke more like an adult to him. "I said no, thank you. Listen, I'm very busy here and . . . well, you know, Wolfgang, maybe you ought to think about looking up some of your old friends. . . . See, there really is only so much you can do here . . . and I'm about . . ." She stopped herself, biting her lip. "Never mind. I don't want any tea."

I put my hand over my mouth to keep from laughing and giving myself away. Good, ya rat, I thought.

Then he wheeled over to where Monica was giving herself a manicure.

"How 'bout you, Mon?" he said. "Some nice Earl Grey?"

"Wolf," she sighed. "I do wish you'd stop asking me if I want tea."

The honeymoon was apparently over.

"But I thought you always liked—"

"It's not the tea, all right?" she yelled.

"Monica!" her mother scolded.

Suddenly I had the feeling I was in the middle of a family thing that I didn't want to see. But I was stuck.

"Well then, can I rub that cream on your feet again?" he said.

That was quite enough now. This was unbearable. It was way, way beyond the point of even being funny.

"Wolfgang, go home," Monica said in a very tired voice. As if she'd said it before.

He bowed his head. As if he'd heard it before too.

I came here for a laugh. This wasn't it.

"Wicked," I blurted.

Everyone turned toward the mirror—toward me. Oops.

Ah, what the heck.

"Wicked! I was right all along. Wicked, wicked, wicked. Who do you think you are, talking to him like that?"

They were all backing away from the mirror now, staring at it up and down, like I was some kind of all-powerful talking volcano or something.

How cool.

I got louder. "You have no right talking to him like that," I boomed. "He may be a chump some-times—"

"Chump?" Wolf objected.

Monica's face brightened. "Johnny! Johnny Chesthair! What a pleasant surprise to have you here, hiding like a rodent within our humble walls."

"I'm not hiding," I said.

Wolf cut in, concerned with only one thing. "How long have you been here?"

I couldn't resist. "Shaddup and fetch me a cup of tea, you."

At least I brought out some of the old Wolf.

"Fetch you a . . . I'll fetch you a cup of *teeth*," he said, waving a fist in the general direction of my voice. "Come out where I can see you, ya coward."

"If I come out," I asked, "will you rub cream on my feet?"

He shot back, "No, but I'll rub your face on the sidewalk."

I laughed mightily.

The woman who was getting her hair done started putting on her coat. She still had the smock on, and her hair was half cut.

Yvette rushed to the mirror. "You, get out of my walls. The two of you macho, macho men, take it outside."

"With pleasure," we both said at once.

I scrambled to get out of my cramped space, the tension and excitement of the moment causing my chest to swell up to three times its regular barrel size. I saw Wolf whiz past on his way out the aquamarine door.

"Hey," I called. "Wait up. I'm stuck. My chest is too big."

It would be just my luck that he didn't hear me, but Monica did. She walked right over to the opening in the wall, stared down my secret passageway, and grinned. "I could come in there and help you," she said.

"I'd rather let the termites eat me," I answered.

"I know why you were here," she said.

"I came to laugh at you two, that's why," I said. "Ha-ha-ha. See. Now I can go."

"You came because you were jealous," she said so sweetly, so viciously.

"*Argghhh,*" I groaned as my chest expanded even farther. The two-by-four framework of the wall creaked. But like Samson, I summoned all my might, gave a great heave, and shoved my way out.

"Let's see any girl do *that*," I bragged.

"Right, let's see any girl get herself *stuck* inside a wall first. Ya macho moron."

Obviously, we had nothing more to discuss. I stormed out.

"Hey," she said from behind, "have a cookie before you go? You're going to need all the strength you can get."

I did not have a chance to respond. As soon as I crossed into the alley, Wolfgang had me by the shirt. "You don't have enough cookies to save this boy, Monica."

"Oh really," I said, grabbing him by his shirt. We remained like that, yakking at each other and barking at Monica at the same time.

"I cannot believe this," she said. "I always figured this was, like, a TV thing, that actual humans— even boys—could never be this boneheaded. . . ."

"Well, you were wrong, weren't you," I said defiantly.

"Good one, bonehead," Wolf said.

"Why don't you both just admit it? The reason for this, for everything that has happened, is very simple: You are both in love with me."

Wolf and I both turned to stare at her while still clutching each other.

"And Steven is so jealous, he's willing to act like an idiot for everyone to see."

I started to say something to her, but Wolf cut me off. He even let go of me so he could be dramatic with his hands, the fool.

"First," he said, sounding more like his old self with every word, "Steven has never had any trouble acting like an idiot for the world to see. And second, he is jealous, but it's not over you, it's over *me*."

I didn't even absorb it right away.

"Ya," I said to Monica. When she began howling with laughter, I replayed the tape in my head.

I turned my full attention on Wolfgang now. With every ounce of me, I threw my free hand into his chest with such menace, my whole arm went numb.

"You mental case!" I said as I watched his

wheelchair tip completely over backward.

He lay on the ground.

Laughing.

There are a few absolute, unbreakable rules, even in the *mano a mano* combat world of men killing men. It is always very bad form to hit a wheelchair-bound person. And you never ever kick a man when he's down. These are pretty universally accepted rules.

I kicked him in the ribs.

We both laughed. Nuts, huh?

I kicked him again, but this time he was ready. He grabbed my foot and started twisting, over and over and over, like on the nature programs when the crocodile is wrestling something into the Nile.

"You two make me want to throw up," Monica snapped, and started back through the aquamarine door.

"Well, good," I said, choking Wolf as we lay grappling in the gutter. "Finally, we're even."

Just before she slammed the door, Wolf got in the last word, as he always does. "Now look who's jealous."

She left us there, on the pavement, whaling on each other. Smiling. Killing each other. Laughing.

11
Our Nuke-u-lar Family

As I rode on the handlebars of Wolfgang's wheel-chair—feeling my swollen lip, admiring the big red apple growing out of his forehead—I was thinking how great it was going to be to have the old unit all together again.

"The guys are going to be so psyched to have you back," I said to him as we pulled up in front of Lars's. "You wait out here. I'm going to warm them up, and I'll call you when it's time to surprise them."

Wolf shrugged. "Sounds a little weenie to me, but I'll go for it. Just don't keep me waiting too long, or I'm outta here."

Right, I thought. Like, where are you gonna go?

"And what's that funny smell?" he asked as I unlocked the door.

I had no time for funny smells. As I stepped inside, I leaned back against the door. What am I doing? They are going to think I've lost my mind completely. The guys? The guys are going to be so psyched? What was I thinking? The guys are terrified of him. And never mind the guys, what are the GALS going to say?

Hey. What *is* that smell?

Oh my god?

I rushed into my club. Holy smokes, I was only gone for a little while. . . .

There was a boom box sitting on top of Lars's tool cabinet, playing dance music. My car—I ran to my car and threw myself on the hood, stroking it like it was an injured animal I found by the side of the road. "You poor thing, what have they done?" What they had done was, they put curtains up all around the inside of the windows. They had put what smelled like a whole case of air fresheners inside. I threw open the door. "Oh my god, oh my god," I said again.

"Do you *mind*?" one of the six—count 'em, *six*—Girl Scouts gathered inside said to me. "We are *trying* to conduct a meeting here."

THEREWASAGIRLSCOUTMEETING-HAPPENINGINMYCAR!!!!!!!!!!!!INMY-CARINMYCARMYJOHNNYCHESTHAIR-MOBILE!!!!!!!!!!!!!!!MYCARMYCARTHE-CENTEROFTHEENTIREJOHNNYCHEST-HAIRUNIVERSE!!!

Girl Scouts. Crammed into my car. Sipping tea. Getting cookie crumbs all over the upholstery.

This would be the equivalent of showing dirty movies in a church.

I rushed around looking for answers. My men? Where were my men?

I'll tell you where.

Ling was lying in the hairdo chair with his face covered in green gunk. Nessy was applying the gunk.

"That's right," Jerome was telling her. "The facial should feel as good to the person who is applying it as it does to the person receiving it."

"My hands do feel a lot softer," said Nessy.

They had set up a second chair—business was so good—where Jerome was now working on Rock's hair.

"Oh, I can see it now," Jerome said. "When you do corn rows, the thing to remember is to pull the strands harder than regular braids, and to keep this center strand over like this the whole time. . . ."

Even my nightmares never went this far.

Wolfgang had by now let himself in and joined the party. Oddly, his appearance caused not a ripple in the room.

"Now I know what that smell is," Wolfgang said,

barely able to form words through his laughter. "It's aromatherapy."

I myself was beyond attempting words. *"Ahhh!"* I screamed. *"Ahhh! Ahhh! Ahhh!"*

"Yes, I see what you mean," Wolf said calmly. "They have taken one of the butchest operations in He-Man history and turned it into a . . ."

He let it hang there on purpose, to torture me.

"Ahhh!" I continued. *"Ahh! Ahh! Ahh!"*

"Y'know, what y'all need," said Cecil, leafing through a booklet, "is some . . . tea tree and ylang-ylang. That's for treating shock." He nearly toppled over trying to pronounce ylang-ylang. "And then some frankincense for stability, some chamomile for your tantrum problem . . ."

"My club!" I yelled. "What have you done to my *cluuuuuuub*?"

"And some sandalwood and tangerine to help you stop living in the past. Sit right on down there, Steven. We'll fix ya right up."

I did. I did sit right down. Beaten. Broken. I plopped down on the garage floor holding my nose, closing my eyes, trying to figure a way to cover my ears with my feet.

Wolf wheeled up beside me, putting a hand on my shoulder. "Gee, you sure showed me, huh? Stealing all my members. What a good idea that was."

"But I won, didn't I?" I said, sounding even to myself like a crazy person. "I won. I won. That's the important thing."

"Ya," he said. "You won. See ya, buddy. Have fun with *your* club."

"Wait!" I said, scrambling after him, not begging, exactly, but dangerously close. "Do something. You have to do something. Can you do something?"

"Of course I can," he said. "Just let me handle it. And whatever I say, just don't disagree."

If that wasn't a windup for a sucker punch, I don't know what is. But I was in a spot.

Casually, Wolf turned from me to the assembled masses.

"Attention, everyone," he yelled. All activity stopped, just like it does in the zebra pack when the lions cruise by. "Steven here has seen the light of day, and brought me back as president of the He-Man Women Haters Club."

"Hey," I said.

"Go have a cookie and shaddup," he said.

There was a groan from the crowd.

"So," he went on. "As most of you no doubt remember from the last club we were in together, there will be an initiation ceremony."

The groaning grew louder.

"All of you who are not original charter members of the HMWHC will now line up over here for the official 'Kissing of the President' procession."

"You are such an embarrassment," I said.

Even the groaning stopped. The Scout meeting inside the Lincoln broke up like a cookie in milk. The owner of the boom box yanked the plug out of the wall and hoisted the thing on her shoulder. Vanessa wiped her hands off on Ling's shirt, and Rock stood up with her half a head of corn rows and made for the door. They marched out single file like a colony of ants.

Wolfgang. As he had done so many times before, one way or another, he'd changed the world by merely opening his mouth. And, as usual, he was enjoying every bit of it.

"What?" he called, wheeling after them. "Was it something I said? I know, you can't decide who goes first, right? You're rushing out for some breath mints, is that it? Hey! It's okay, go on and fight over me. I'll kiss the winner and losers, I don't mind—"

Slam! They were gone.

I went right over to Wolfgang and shook his hand, laughing. He basked in his ability to clear a room.

Over in the corner the He-Men stood expressionless.

"What about you guys?" I said. "You must have something to say."

Jerome spoke for all of them. He shrugged. "Who wants a haircut?"

"That's it? What about this?" I pointed at Wolf. "Aren't you shocked?"

"Shocked? Steven, we are not shocked. We are He-Men."

"Ya," Ling said. "We figured out about two weeks ago that you were trying to get him back."

"Ahhh!" I said. *"Ahhh!"*

"Never figured you was gonna make him boss again, though," Cecil said.

"Oh, no, that part was just a ploy to scare the girls out," I assured them.

"Ploy, nothing," Wolfgang said. "That was my fee for getting rid of them. I'm the Man again."

"What?" I protested. "No. No. No way. This is my club, and besides, you think these guys are going to have you back again after all you've . . . ?"

I looked to the guys. All three shrugged.

"Would you stop doing that, please?" I snapped.

Jerome, my oldest and dearest compatriot, came over to reassure me. "Steven," he said, punching my shoulder, "does it really matter, with this bunch, who's in charge? Is that really the important thing with us?"

Jerome was still able to make me feel stupid more than the rest. And considering how all the worst things always seemed to happen as a result of my lust for power . . . I was feeling extra foolish now.

"Ya, you're right," I said, turning to shake Wolf's hand once again like this was the official ceremony ending a very cool and important war. "What matters is that the He-Man Women Haters Club is together, not who's in charge of it."

Lying my hairy butt off. Of course it mattered. It mattered a whole lot. And the first chance I got . . .

Don't miss the other books in the
He-Man Women Haters Club
Series!

The He-Man Women Haters Club #1—
JOHNNY CHESTHAIR

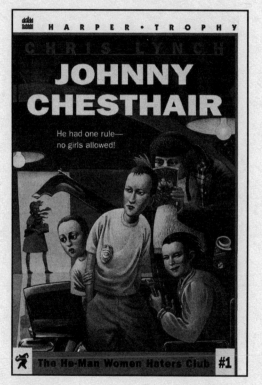

The He-Man Women Haters Club
#2—

The He-Man Women Haters Club #2—

BABES IN THE WOODS

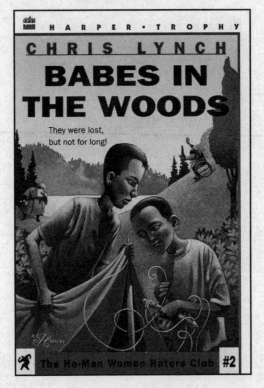

The He-Man Women Haters Club #3—

SCRATCH AND THE SNIFFS

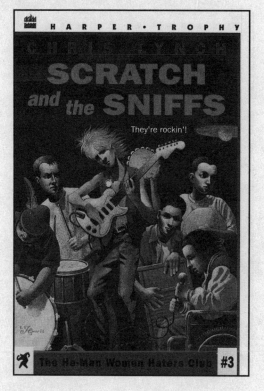

The He-Man Women Haters Club #4—
LADIES' CHOICE